PASSING THROUGH

Story by Carmel Reilly
Illustrations by Deborah Hinde

NELSON
CENGAGE Learning

Passing Through

Text: Carmel Reilly
Series consultant: Annette Smith
Publishing editor: Simone Calderwood
Editor: Ted Carisbrooke
Project editor: Annabel Smith
Designer: James Lowe
Series designers: James Lowe and
    Karen Mayo
Illustrations: Deborah Hinde
Production controller: Erin Dowling

PM Guided Reading
Sapphire Level 30

Text © 2016 Cengage Learning Australia Pty Limited
Illustrations © 2016 Cengage Learning Australia Pty Limited

ISBN 978 0 17 037952 6

Cengage Learning Australia
Level 7, 80 Dorcas Street
South Melbourne, Victoria Australia 3205
Phone: 1300 790 853

Cengage Learning New Zealand
Unit 4B Rosedale Office Park
331 Rosedale Road, Albany, North Shore NZ 0632
Phone: 0800 449 725

For learning solutions, visit **cengage.com.au**

Printed in China by 1010 Printing International Ltd
1 2 3 4 5 6 7 20 19 18 17 16

CONTENTS

Chapter 1
THE BIG CITY

Lewis sat in the passenger's seat of the car as it sped away from the airport, onto the freeway that headed towards the city.

He stared out at the unfamiliar landscape – flat, yellow countryside out one window, vast car parks for the airport out the other.

The road unrolled in front of them like a thick strap of liquorice. Cars, trucks and motorbikes whizzed past in both directions.

"I don't suppose you have so many cars up where you live?" said Helen, who was driving.

Lewis, who lived in a small community in remote central Australia, shook his head and laughed. "No, not this many. There are only a few hundred people in Mira River."

"But you've been to the city before, haven't you?" asked Helen.

"I went to Alice Springs for my interview to come here for school," Lewis responded. "But that wasn't really very big."

"No," Helen agreed. "Not compared to Melbourne."

Soon, they turned off the freeway and into the city centre. They passed shops and larger buildings, before turning into another street where the buildings were so high that everything was completely in shadow.

The people on the footpaths nearby all seemed to be in a hurry, with most using their phones. Lewis noticed that, even on a hot day like this one, most of them were wearing dark clothes – even the ones who didn't look like they were going to work.

And everyone was wearing shoes. Lewis wiggled his cramped toes inside his runners, and smiled as he thought about pulling his shoes off as soon as he could.

"These buildings are tall, aren't they?" said Helen. "Some of them are more than eighty storeys high."

"Eighty storeys …" he echoed, turning his head upwards, and pressing his face to the window to see if he could glimpse the tops of the buildings.

Lewis came from the desert. Everything was flat there as far as the eye could see.

The only buildings at Mira River were all single storey. Even in Alice Springs, the tallest buildings were only a few levels high.

Soon, the car had moved through the dense traffic and out of the city centre. Once again, Lewis could see the sky.

They passed shops, car yards, petrol stations and hotels. Helen told Lewis about his new school and a little bit about her job as a boarding-house supervisor, looking after students like him who came from all over the country.

They drove alongside a park that seemed to stretch for miles. Lewis became distracted and stared out the window. Everywhere he looked, there were people running, people cycling and people walking their dogs.

It occurred to Lewis suddenly that nothing here in the city seemed like home, even though he was still in the same country. It wasn't just that the city was so enormous. It was the colour of the land and the sky, the smells, and the feel of the air around him, as well.

He felt like he was in a foreign place, and he shivered a little at the thought of being so far from home. Everything felt different. Weird.

But then, everything had been feeling weird in one way or another since he'd stepped into the truck yesterday morning … even since before then, really, if he thought about it.

Perhaps since his mum first mentioned the idea of going to boarding school in Melbourne last year – since she suggested doing something no one else in his family had ever done before.

Chapter 2

BACK HOME

Lewis's mum's name was Tilly. She was a tall, slender woman, with dark, glowing skin and a brilliant smile. When Lewis thought of her, the word "kind" came into his mind. She was the sort of person who never changed, no matter what.

She was almost always cheerful and positive. It wasn't that she didn't become angry sometimes. She would certainly always tell Lewis if she wasn't content with something he'd done – or more likely something he hadn't done. But once she'd let him know this fact, her annoyance passed and she was back to being her usual self again.

Lewis was glad she was his mother. He hadn't seen his dad for years now, and really didn't know him at all. Having one outstanding parent seemed to him to be just as acceptable as having two parents who were merely satisfactory.

For as long as Lewis could remember, his mum had always said that she wanted him to achieve something. "What does that mean?" he asked her, when he was old enough to try and make some sense of what she was saying.

"It means doing something good with your life," said Tilly one day, when they were talking about the future. "You know, when I was young I wanted to be a nurse. But I would have had to go away to study, and Mumma Kath and Pop didn't have the money to pay for me to go down to Brisbane or Sydney to study.

"Then, the time went by and I got married and had children and it was too hard for me to leave ..." Tilly had looked wistfully at the horizon, as though she would still get up and walk into a different life if she had half a chance.

"But I don't know what I want to do," Lewis had said.

"Well, maybe if you went away to a school in a big city you'd get to see all the things you could do," his mum replied.

"But how could I do that?" asked Lewis. "You can't afford to send me away any more than Mumma Kath and Pop could."

Tilly turned to him and smiled. "Well, maybe I can. I've been talking to some people at your school.

Have you ever heard of an education scholarship, Lewis Najama?"

Lewis shook his head. No, he hadn't heard about one of those.

"An education scholarship might be able to pay for you to go to boarding school down south," she said. "Imagine, you could have the same advantages as all those rich people. You could become a lawyer or a doctor."

"A doctor …" Lewis repeated. "Then I could come back and take care of people here."

Chapter 3

WELCOME TO SCHOOL

Lewis was thinking about this conversation with his mum as he drove through the suburbs of Melbourne with Helen. The tree-lined streets were full of comfortable-looking houses with pretty gardens behind wooden fences.

There was nothing like this in Mira River. In Mira River, no one had a garden because the soil was poor, and lack of rain made cultivating most plants almost impossible.

After a few minutes, he saw a high stone fence with a sign that read: "Southward School". Helen slowed the car and pulled into an entrance flanked by huge wrought-iron gates. "Here we are," said Helen, as she proceeded up the driveway towards a cluster of impressive-looking buildings.

"Look at that," said Lewis, noting the immense playing fields on their left. "That is the greenest grass I have ever seen."

At home, the grounds Lewis played on were dry, dusty expanses of dirt where only the occasional clump of grass grew. He'd never played on soft-looking grass like this. He imagined it tickling the soles of his feet.

"There are great sports facilities here," said Helen. "We have a pool, a gym and two indoor basketball courts. You will love it."

Helen drove up to a red-brick building that looked like a large old house. It had a steep, tiled roof and orange–green ivy growing across its facade. Helen explained that this building was the main office.

Inside, Lewis met the principal, Ms Oates, who welcomed him to the school. Then, Mr Sayers appeared. He was the person who had interviewed Lewis for his scholarship in Alice Springs.

"Hello, Lewis!" Mr Sayers beamed. "I'm so glad to see you again."

Lewis smiled back shyly. A part of him wanted to say he was glad, too, but another part of him wasn't really sure.

It had been early that morning when Lewis last saw his mum as she waved him off at the departure gates at the airport. And it had been a whole day since he'd left his home, and his sisters and brother. In his mind's eye, he saw his family looking at him, their faces stained with tears.

"When are you going to come back?" his brother had asked between sobs.

"I won't be away too long," Lewis had replied, because saying "nine weeks" didn't mean anything to a five-year-old. He'd had to bite his lip to stop himself from crying, too.

Lewis tried to put his family out of his mind and concentrate on what Mr Sayers and Ms Oates were saying about the school and about all the opportunities he would have.

When the welcome session finished, Lewis got into the car with Helen. They drove back outside the gates and around the corner into a side street.

"This is your new abode!" exclaimed Helen, as they pulled to a stop outside a big, old two-storey building.

Lewis frowned. "What's an abode?" he asked.

"A place to live," said Helen.

They got out of the car and Lewis retrieved his bags from the boot. "There are so many words I don't know. At home we speak two languages. Warlpiri is my first language. I learnt proper English at school, but I worry that I don't know as much as the other kids here."

"You'll catch up quickly," said Helen. "I didn't grow up speaking English at home either."

"Really?" said Lewis, as he followed Helen to the front door. "What language did you speak?"

Helen opened the door. "Greek," she said. "I never spoke a word of English until I was five. You'd never know now, would you?"

She smiled at Lewis, and together they carried his belongings upstairs to his new room.

Chapter 4
TOO QUIET

It was two days before school began. Lewis was going to be sharing his room in the boarding house with another boy, but he hadn't arrived yet. In fact, Lewis was the first person at the house, apart from Helen, who had a room downstairs, and another supervisor called Mark.

Lewis unpacked his things, shoving most of them into a set of drawers between the two beds. He didn't have many possessions. He would have to go to the school uniform shop tomorrow to collect his uniform, which he saw from the list was very expensive. He was extremely grateful that his scholarship was going to pay for it all.

When he had finished unpacking, he realised he was really hungry. Helen said the dining hall that all the boarders went to during term time wasn't open yet, so tonight Mark would cook dinner in the kitchen downstairs.

Mark prepared a dish called risotto, which was a wet, thick rice with pieces of chicken and pumpkin in it, and a big green salad.

At home, Lewis mostly ate plain food, such as meat, potatoes and bread, and sometimes he'd have bush foods, like kangaroo, or root vegetables, berries and seeds that Mumma Kath and the old aunties would go out and collect.

Lewis had never had anything like risotto before, and he was impressed. He hoped the food in the dining room would be as delicious.

After dinner, Lewis realised he was feeling extraordinarily tired. "I know it's been a very long day for you," said Helen. "Why don't you just go up to your room?"

Upstairs, Lewis changed and got into bed. He quickly turned off the bedside lamp, expecting that the darkness would quickly pull him into sleep. After a minute, he noticed that light was coming in around the edges of the curtain from the street lamp outside.

The light made him aware of the room and everything around him, such as the wardrobe doors and the chest of drawers. But the more he looked around, the more he saw dark, menacing shadows and strange shapes. He was sure that something near the bedroom door was moving. His heart beat fast and he flicked on the light – only to see a long coat hanging limply from a hook.

Lewis sighed with relief. "Don't be silly," he told himself.

He turned the light off again and closed his eyes. Everything was quiet. Occasionally he could hear the hum of a car passing on the main road around the corner, but mostly there was an eerie stillness around him.

He was accustomed to sharing a room and hearing the groans and snorts of his brother and sisters sleeping. He was used to hearing the yapping and howling of the town dogs that roamed the streets at night.

Sometimes, there were parties or people out on the road talking or arguing. Mira River might be remote, but it was not quiet.

Nor was it a place where he ever felt alone. At Mira River, he was always with family. Everyone who lived there was related to him in some way. If his mum went somewhere, he always had Mumma Kath to go to, or Aunty Gracie or Aunty Lal or Uncle Kep. He had all his cousins to play with.

Footy could be a non-stop game at Mira River, with different kids coming and going all day.

He'd only been gone a day, but it felt like an eternity. How long would nine weeks feel like? How long a year, and then another five years after that? *There was no way he was going to last here,* he thought. He wanted to go home now.

Or at least first thing tomorrow morning.

Chapter 5

A NEW ROOM-MATE

When Lewis woke, it took him only a few seconds to remember where he was. He leaned across his bed and pushed the curtains to one side. The sun was already high in the sky and, from his room, he could see out across the school and the surrounding rooftops.

Lewis wasn't feeling as bad as he had been the night before. Instead, he felt just a little excited, wondering what the day might bring.

After he'd showered and had breakfast, he noticed the boarding house was starting to get busy with parents dropping off children.

Lewis stood at the front door for a while, searching the crowds as they passed, hoping to see some faces like his own. But while he saw a few different nationalities, he didn't see anyone who looked Indigenous. Although he had been told there were other Indigenous kids at school, so far he hadn't seen any at all.

Just before lunch, Lewis went with Mark to get his uniform, trying on all the pieces to check the sizes were right. He smiled at his reflection in the mirror and wished his mum could see how great he looked in his new clothes.

After lunch, he practised kicking goals with Mark, using a football from the sports room.

After an hour, they finished, and Lewis went back to his room. Lewis's room-mate had arrived and was putting his things away. He seemed surprised when he saw Lewis standing at the door.

"Are you looking for someone?" the boy asked.

"No, this is my room, too," said Lewis, pointing to his bed. "I'm Lewis."

"Oh!" said the boy, looking a little annoyed. "Is that all your stuff in the drawers? You need to move it. I don't have enough space."

Lewis looked away from the boy, feeling slightly irritated, but not wanting to have a disagreement when they had only just met.

Lewis pulled his things from one of the drawers and threw them on his bed. He could see the boy had twice as many clothes as he had, as well as a lot of books and electronic games.

All the boy's things looked new, as if they had

been bought for him just to come to school.

Then Mark appeared at the door. "Hey," he said. "I see you boys have met each other. Good. I wanted to let you know that dinner is in the dining hall tonight at 6 pm sharp." Then he looked over at Lewis, sitting on his bed. "And you'll need to put away all those clothes first, Lewis."

Lewis wanted to say he didn't have anywhere to put them, but then he saw the other boy had folded his clothes extremely neatly. He thought perhaps if he folded his clothes neatly, too, he could fit everything into one drawer. After all, he didn't need nearly as much space.

Mark spoke again. "Did you put the football back in the sports room, Lewis?"

Lewis looked up. "Oh! I left it on the field," he said. "I didn't know I was meant to put it away."

"You should have returned it to the same place it came from," said Mark.

"At home, we just leave the footy out for the next person to come along and play with," said Lewis.

The boy next to him made a strange gurgling sound at the back of his throat, like a laugh he was trying to suppress.

"Oliver!" Mark snapped at Lewis's room-mate.

"You can be helpful by going back to school with Lewis to help him find the ball."

"If it's still there," replied Oliver in a flat voice.

Oliver didn't say anything to Lewis as they trooped downstairs and walked across the path. It wasn't until they were on the sports field that Oliver finally spoke. "Where did you leave it?" he asked.

"Just by the goal posts over there," replied Lewis.

They looked around the oval, but the football had disappeared.

"I knew that would happen," said Oliver. "You'll have to pay for that ball now."

"Really?" said Lewis.

"Yeah," said Oliver. "You get in a lot of trouble when you lose the school's equipment. You'll get a black mark on your record."

"What's a black mark?" asked Lewis.

"They're like points against you, and if you get too many of them, the school will expel you," replied Oliver, knowingly.

As they walked back to the boarding house, Lewis felt nauseous. It was only his first day here and he had lost a ball and would probably receive a black mark. He didn't have much money with him. How could he put this right?

It had cost Lewis's family everything they could spare to fly him down to Melbourne. His school and the local bank had set up a fund to assist him with his scholarship, and people at Mira River had donated money as well.

Lewis felt terrible that people had given him so much and he might have let them down. How could he pay for the football?

He had only about ten dollars in his bag back in his room. Would that be enough?

And what about the black mark? Was there any way that he could get rid of that? How many would he have to get to be expelled?

Lewis felt a rush of homesickness. He wanted nothing more than to be back in Mira River with his family and friends, but he couldn't go back in disgrace. He would have to find a way to sort this out first.

Chapter 6
NEW FRIENDS

Lewis was worried. He decided to run up to his room and check how much money he had, but as he turned to walk towards the house, Helen appeared suddenly.

"We're going to the dining hall now, Lewis. It's this way," she said, with a big smile. Then, she saw Lewis's worried face. "Is there something wrong?" she asked.

"I lost a football," he said. "I left it on the sports field and now it's gone."

"Don't worry. Someone will have picked it up and returned it to the sports room."

"But if it's lost, I have to pay for it! And I don't have much money with me."

"Nonsense. You won't have to pay for it," said Helen, frowning.

"But I'm going to get a black mark!"

Helen looked blankly at him. "What's a black mark?" she asked.

"You get them when you do bad things and then you get expelled," said Lewis.

Helen raised her eyebrows. "I don't know where you got that information from, but it is completely wrong. Listen, Lewis, if you have any concerns about anything, come to me. All right?"

"All right," he echoed.

Lewis walked into the dining hall. The place was full. He scanned the room and saw Oliver, who had already taken a seat across at the far table. He was with another boy and they were laughing.

Lewis felt his face grow hot with shame and anger. He looked away, searching the room again for a place to sit.

"There is a gap just over here," said Mark, who was standing behind him.

Mark shepherded him over to a table of boys and girls. They all looked about his age. It was clear that none of them knew each other very well. They looked up when Lewis arrived, and Mark introduced him to them above the noise.

One of the girls patted the seat next to her. "You can sit here," she smiled.

As soon as he had sat down, the boy across from him said, curiously, "Where are you from?"

The boy had never heard of Mira River, so Lewis had to tell him where it was. He told him a little about his life in the outback.

Soon, everyone at the table was interested. One boy talked about how he had driven through the outback with his parents when they had gone to Uluru. A girl mentioned she had been to Kakadu and to Ubirr to see rock art. Lewis said the people at Mira River did a lot of paintings, and added proudly that some of his aunties were quite famous artists these days. Their paintings were in galleries all over Australia.

The food arrived and Lewis began to eat. He felt happier now. He liked the people at his table and they seemed to like him, too. He was pleased to learn that two of the boys, Aiden and Matt, lived in the same boarding house as he did.

After dinner, they walked back from the dining hall together. They invited Lewis into their room and he sat chatting with them until it was time for bed.

They swapped stories about their primary schools. Matt and Aiden had so many facilities and programmes at their primary school. In Year Six, they'd even gone on a school trip to Japan. Japan!

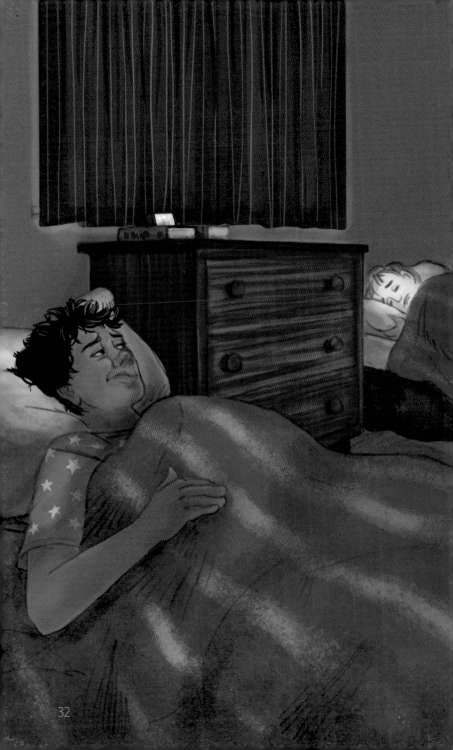

Lewis's only trips out of Mira River were into the desert with his uncles to hunt or to take part in special ceremonies. It felt like a world away.

When Lewis finally returned to his room, he was glad to see that the lights were off and Oliver was already in bed. Lewis got changed in the dark and slid under the covers. His mind drifted to home again. He could see his family, sitting around their old kitchen table, eating and yarning, with everyone laughing. He felt his stomach clench with loss.

Then, as he lay listening to the silence of the night, he heard something. It was a strange kind of whimpering, like the sound his dogs at home made when they were afraid. He held his breath for a moment and concentrated. There it was again. The noise seemed to be coming from the other side of the room. He turned his head slightly. The sound was coming from Oliver.

Chapter 7

SETTLING IN

"Wake up!" someone called. Lewis sat bolt upright, shocked, not knowing where he was.

Mark stood over him. "You slept through your alarm. You need to get up straight away. I'm surprised Oliver didn't make sure you were up."

Lewis pulled his uniform from the cupboard and threw on a shirt and shorts, and shoes and socks. He had missed breakfast. He rushed straight over to the school gymnasium where the first-year students, like him, were having their orientation session. He managed to join the group just as they were sitting down.

The teachers spoke about what to expect in the year to come. Then they took the students around the school on an orientation tour. At the end, the students were assigned to their home classrooms. Lewis was pleased to discover that both Aiden and Matt were in his class, and that Oliver was not.

The day passed quickly. There was a lot to do.

At lunchtime, Mr Sayers approached Lewis.

"Hi, Lewis," he said. "Don't forget there's an Indigenous students' meeting in my office in fifteen minutes."

Lewis was surprised. He didn't remember Mr Sayers mentioning that. His grade six teacher at Mira River was always telling him to focus harder and concentrate more. Sometimes he was easily distracted. He knew he would have to try and remember everything that people said to him. Southward School was a place with a very full timetable. There was always so much happening, in classes and at lunchtime – and after school. He couldn't afford to miss anything.

Mr Sayers' office was full when Lewis arrived. There were many more Indigenous students than he'd imagined. They were in every year level, and most of them looked older than him. He could see that many of them knew each other from the way they were sitting around in small groups, laughing and talking.

"Everyone! This is Lewis, one of our new first years," said Mr Sayers over the din.

They all stopped talking at once and looked at Lewis.

"Hi! Hello! Hi!" came a chorus of voices.

"Welcome to school!" cried an older girl at the back of the room.

A boy who looked a few years older than him tilted his head to Lewis. "Come and sit with us," he said. "I'm Kyle, this is Jenna and Mac. How are you enjoying school so far?"

Lewis screwed up his face. "It's … I don't know. It's hard to explain."

They all laughed. "Not to us," said Jenna. "Believe me, everything that you've experienced, we have, too. Where are you from, anyway?"

Lewis told them.

Jenna grinned. "I'm from the Torres Strait Islands. I've come even further than you! Not that I'm competing or anything."

Everyone laughed.

"It's lonely to begin with," said Jenna. "No one understands how important family is. But, you know, you get used to it. I've even learned to like it here, especially the swimming pool and the library! And you make good friends."

"Hey," said Kyle. "I think we're in the same boarding house. I'm downstairs, so I can help you whenever you need something."

Lewis looked around. "Mr Sayers said there was another first-year student, but I haven't seen anyone else that looks new like me."

Mac shrugged. "Maybe they're not here yet. Some people arrive late."

Everyone laughed again.

Lewis looked puzzled.

"Getting to places on time might be something you struggle with here at first," said Jenna. "We've all experienced this. It can be difficult waking so early in the morning and arriving to class on time. 'Being punctual', they call it. It's so much more relaxed at home. In the country, we say, 'What's the rush?'"

Lewis nodded. "Yes, it's the same at my home, too. We don't live by the clock. No one wears a watch."

"It's different here," said Mac. "Everyone is in a big hurry. There's so much to fit in. It's hard, but in the long term, it is worth it. You will learn an incredible amount. And you will get amazing opportunities here. My brother has just started university. And I'm planning to go to university, too. What about you? What do you want to do?"

Lewis nodded. "I want to go to university. I want to be a doctor."

"Well," said Mac. "You're going to have to work really hard. But this is the right place for you."

When the bell rang, Lewis didn't want to leave. He hurried off towards the central building where he knew his next class was, hoping he remembered the room.

Lewis soon saw Matt, who waved to him. "Over here," Matt said, and they walked to class together.

At the end of the day, Lewis was feeling a lot better about being at school. He had been so busy he'd barely had time to think.

As well as going to English, Maths and Japanese classes, he also had his first period of Sport.

It felt good to be running around outside, and it felt good to be in comfortable clothes again after the restrictions of the normal uniform.

Wearing that uniform is going to be the worst thing about school, Lewis thought.

That, and sharing a room with Oliver.

Chapter 8

STRANGE NOISES

When Lewis went up to his room after dinner, the space was empty. He had just settled down on his bed when the door burst open and Oliver walked in with another boy.

"Hello," said the new boy. "You must be Oliver's room-mate."

"Yes, I'm Lewis."

"I'm Harry," said the boy.

"Look at this, Harry," said Oliver, ignoring Lewis and walking over to his bed where he picked up his laptop.

Harry and Oliver sat on the edge of the bed and watched something on the screen. Lewis waited for a moment to see if he was invited, but it was clear they weren't even thinking about him, so he went downstairs to the common room where he was relieved to find Matt and Aiden playing a game of table soccer.

"Come and join us," said Matt.

At bedtime, Lewis headed back upstairs. Harry had gone now and Oliver was still looking at his computer.

"Hi," said Lewis, trying to break the ice.

"Hmm," Oliver grunted, looking glum.

Lewis left the room to brush his teeth. When he came back, Oliver went to brush his teeth. Lewis got into bed and turned the light out. A few minutes later, he heard Oliver come into the room and soon he had turned his light out, too.

Once again, Lewis lay in the almost-darkness and thoughts whizzed round and round in his head. At home, he normally fell asleep quickly, but here in the boarding house, he was having a lot of trouble. And he had to get up so early in the mornings.

It made him feel anxious thinking about that, and all he had to do. There was homework and sports practice and making sure he kept all his clothes clean and tidy. He wanted to go home.

He wanted to see his mum and his brother – and even his sisters, who usually annoyed him more than anyone!

He thought about all the study he had to do to get into university to study medicine. He would make his family so proud. But how long would he have to be away? Years and years. Was it worth it?

He was so busy thinking about all these things that it took him a while to realise that Oliver was making that sound again. Perhaps he was sick? Lewis wasn't sure what to do. He lay still and listened and after a minute he said, "Are you all right?"

There was a loud hiccupping sound. "Yes," Oliver hissed. "Leave me alone."

"Okay," said Lewis, feeling confused.

The noise seemed to stop then, although Lewis thought he could hear the occasional gulping sound as he finally drifted off to sleep.

● ● ●

The next morning, Lewis saw Helen while he was doing his clean-up duties.

"You look rather tired," she said. "Are you sleeping properly?"

"Not really. I'm not used to getting up so early. And it's difficult to get off to sleep, too."

"Is something keeping you awake?" asked Helen. "Are you homesick?"

Lewis frowned. "A bit. But it's not just that. Oliver makes noises."

"What kind of noises? Do you mean snoring?"

"No, weird noises that sound like dogs whining. I asked him if he was okay and he told me to go away."

"Hmm," said Helen. "Thanks for telling me."

Lewis's eyes opened wide. "Don't tell him I said anything. I don't want him to think I'm talking about him behind his back."

Helen smiled. "I won't breathe a word."

Chapter 9

FRIDAY NIGHT

It was Friday night dinner, and Lewis was in the food queue when he heard a voice behind him.

It was Kyle. "Hi Lewis, how are you going?" he asked.

Lewis was tired. He hadn't slept well all week. And he was unhappy, too. He had an unfriendly room-mate and a mountain of work to catch up on if he wanted to get top marks. He looked at the ground and tried not to cry.

"Hey, hey … I can see you're not so good," said Kyle. "Come and talk to me after dinner, okay?"

Lewis nodded.

He went and sat down with Aiden and Matt. They were excited about a computer game they liked to play, called Zoomtron.

Lewis had never heard of Zoomtron. He didn't have a laptop, or a tablet or even a phone, like most of the other kids.

Lewis hadn't even used a computer much before he came here. They only had two at his primary school in Mira River. Everyone had to take turns using the one in his classroom and it had broken down a few times.

Lewis looked around the room. He saw Oliver in the far corner. He was usually with Harry, but tonight Harry didn't seem to be around. Then, he realised the dining room was only half-full because some of the students had gone home for the weekend.

"Do you like Zoomtron?" Aiden asked Lewis.

Lewis explained to his new friends that he had never played it.

"You can come and play it with us," said Matt. "You can use one of the computers in the common room and we can all play together."

"What about your room-mate?" Aiden asked, pointing at Oliver. "Does he play? He could join us."

Lewis looked over at Oliver, who was still barely speaking to him. "No, he won't want to play."

After dinner, Lewis went up to his room. He was surprised to find Oliver there at his desk, a pile of maths books in front of him.

Lewis was confused. For a moment, he just stood

there and stared. He wasn't going to say anything, but then he couldn't help blurting out, "You're doing maths on a Friday night!"

"That's right," said Oliver, tersely.

When they'd been doing their homework in the evenings, Lewis hadn't looked at Oliver's work before. But this time, he noticed some of the books were four levels higher than the work they were doing in class. He stared for a moment.

"You don't need to stand there like that, do you?" said Oliver.

"You're on a high level," said Lewis. "You must be really smart."

"So what!" Oliver snapped, turning to look at Lewis, his cheeks red and his eyes watering. "Just leave me alone."

"Okay!" said Lewis, putting his hands up in a sign of surrender. He grabbed a jumper from the cupboard and walked out of the room.

In the hallway outside, he slumped up against the wall and pressed his eyes shut. It was hard to believe how hostile Oliver was and how bad it made him feel.

If he had a phone, he would have called home. But his mum didn't have a phone either, so it would be hard to arrange a call. Besides, it would only worry her.

He needed to talk to someone to help him sort everything out. He thought about Kyle's offer, and ran downstairs to his room and knocked on the door. But there was no answer. As he stood there wondering what to do, Helen walked past.

"Hello," she said. "I've been looking for you. I thought we could have a review of your first week. Are you free now? Do you want to come and have a chat in my office?"

"All right," said Lewis, following her along the hallway.

Helen asked Lewis a few questions about his lessons and settling in at school.

"And how are you getting on with your room-mate, Oliver?"

Lewis took a deep breath. Although he had problems with Oliver, he didn't want to get him into trouble or make the situation worse. "He's all right," he said, after a long pause.

Helen leaned forward. "That pause tells me you are not getting along very well. You said the other day he was making funny noises in his sleep. What else is going on?"

Lewis shrugged. "I don't know. He doesn't talk to me."

"He must have said a few things to you," said Helen, frowning. "You are sharing a room, after all."

"Not really," said Lewis.

Helen thought for a moment. "How would you feel if we moved you to another room?"

Lewis's face lit up. "That would be excellent!"

Helen nodded. "I wasn't sure about the two of you sharing a room. You've both got a lot of adjusting to do. We thought you might get on really well, but maybe it's just too difficult."

"What kind of adjusting does Oliver have to do?" said Lewis. "He's got so many things, and he's really intelligent. I don't understand."

"Sometimes there are things about people that we can't know or understand when we just look at them," said Helen.

Lewis nodded. He knew how true that was.

"What do you think about having a chat with Oliver?" asked Helen.

Lewis shook his head. "I don't want any trouble. Can't you just move me out of that room so I'll never have to see him again?"

Helen smiled gently. "There won't be trouble. Before I think about moving either of you, I think we need to sort a few things out, that's all."

Lewis looked disappointed.

"You don't want to run away from awkward situations," Helen went on. "You need to find out what's going on. You and Oliver will be at school together for the next six years; you can't avoid each other forever."

Reluctantly, Lewis followed Helen back upstairs.

Helen knocked lightly on the bedroom door, but there was no reply. Lewis opened it quietly. The lights inside were off and Oliver seemed to be asleep.

Chapter 10

A GOOD SPORT

When Lewis woke the next morning, Oliver was gone. Lewis checked the clock and saw it was 8.15 am. He tidied his bed, pulled on his sports uniform and raced downstairs and over to the dining room. He joined Kyle at a table to eat breakfast.

"What sport are you playing this term?" asked Kyle.

"Basketball," said Lewis.

"Good," said Kyle. "I'm helping the coach today."

After breakfast, they walked over to the gym together. Inside, about 20 students were milling around, some talking, some taking shots at goals. Helen was there, too, and she waved as they walked in. "I'll be coaching Saturday-morning basketball this term," she said.

Helen and Kyle quickly divided the players into four groups. "There are going to be two teams this semester. We'll use this session to work out who will be in which team," said Helen.

Lewis hadn't noticed Oliver when he first came in, but as Kyle called out people's names, he suddenly realised they were going to be in the same group. Soon they were standing side-by-side, catching and passing balls and taking shots at goals.

Basketball wasn't Lewis's best sport. He'd never had much of a chance to play at Mira River, because they didn't have a proper court. But he liked playing, and he knew that, with a little practice, he could be good at it. He was fast, and he caught and threw the ball well.

Oliver's ball skills were poor by comparison and he moved slowly. For the first time, Lewis realised he had an advantage over Oliver.

He watched as Oliver struggled to catch balls and sometimes miss them altogether. One of the other boys pointed at Oliver as he ran awkwardly to pick up the ball. Another one said loudly that he didn't want Oliver to be on his team.

Lewis was almost going to add a negative comment, too, when he heard his mother's voice in his head – the words she'd said to him as he got on the plane to Melbourne: "Look after yourself and make us proud."

Lewis's mum always told him to ignore people

when they were being mean, and to help people in need. She said people were often mean when they were in need – when they were hurt. Maybe that was Oliver's problem? Whatever it was, Lewis realised that making Oliver look silly wouldn't make his family proud.

When it was his turn to throw the ball to Oliver, Lewis was slow and gentle. He made sure Oliver was ready. When they stood together he told him to move to get the ball, and stepped back to let him catch it. A couple of times Lewis caught the ball and quickly flicked it on to Oliver. He saw a look cross Oliver's face. It wasn't exactly gratitude, but it was an acknowledgement. Oliver realised that Lewis was helping him out.

After basketball, Lewis lost sight of Oliver. He walked back to the boarding house with Kyle and then went to have a shower. When he got back, Oliver was sitting on his bed.

"Hi," said Lewis.

Oliver gave him a strange look and then turned away.

"What's the matter?" asked Lewis.

"I think you know," said Oliver. "Trying to make me look stupid. Well, you succeeded."

"What?!" said Lewis, frowning. "I was only trying to help you."

"Sure," replied Oliver, taking out his laptop. "Well, I don't need your help."

Lewis felt his temper fraying. He forced himself to think about his mum again. What would she say if he got into a fight? He had to deal with this in the right way.

It was time to get Helen.

Chapter 11

TIME TO TALK

Helen pulled out the desk chair and sat down.

"I just came to see how everything is with you two," she said. "I hear you boys haven't been talking much."

"We don't have a lot in common," said Oliver.

"Really?" said Helen. "How do you know that if you haven't spoken?"

"I've seen what he's like," said Oliver, his eyes narrowing.

Lewis felt anger simmer inside him. "What do you mean? I've never done anything to you."

"Today you tried to make me look stupid by treating me like a baby at basketball."

Lewis looked to Helen. "I was only trying to help him."

Oliver scoffed. "You, help me! I could tell what kind of a person you were as soon as I first saw you. The first day at school, I was going past the sports fields with my dad and he said 'Look at that boy over there!' My dad loves athletes."

"What's wrong with being an athlete?" said Lewis.

"My dad thinks they are great people just because they are good at sport. But I don't agree. I think they like to be the centre of attention and they get away with all sorts of things because they are seen as 'cool'. But really, most of the time they have no respect for anyone else."

"Well, I'm not like that," said Lewis, indignantly.

"You're really untidy. You leave stuff everywhere. When you got here, you took over all the drawers with your clothes and didn't leave any room for my things," said Oliver. "When I asked you to take stuff out you were really grumpy."

"You tried to take the drawers over!" growled Lewis. "We have to share them."

"Boys!" cried Helen, holding her hands up. "There are obviously some problems here and we need to get to the bottom of them. Now, let's talk quietly about this. Lewis, what do you have to say about all of this?"

Lewis shrugged. "I've tried to be friendly and he's been horrible to me. There's not much more to add."

Helen looked at Oliver. "I know it's hard for you coming here and adjusting. But it's a very difficult time for Lewis, too."

Oliver frowned. "Why would it be hard for him?"

Lewis leaned forward. He could feel tears sting his eyes. "I've never been away from my place before, never been in a big city. There's so much I don't know and I'm behind in my schoolwork. I miss my family and I want to go home, but the people in my community sacrificed a lot for me to come here and I can't let them down. So I'm stuck."

"Well, at least you've got a family who cares about you," said Oliver, petulantly. "You can ring or video call them when you need to."

Lewis let out a loud huff. "My mum doesn't have a phone or a computer, so calling home is not an option."

"Oh," said Oliver, obviously surprised.

"Anyway, you have a family, Oliver," said Helen. "You have your dad."

"He's always away on business," said Oliver. "He doesn't care about me. He's always too busy to call, and when he does he only cares if I've topped the class. And even that's not good enough. He wants me to be sporty as well." Oliver leaned forward with his lip quivering.

Suddenly, Lewis realised Oliver's lips weren't twitching in annoyance. Oliver was trying to stop himself from crying. The strange sounds he'd heard in the night were Oliver's stifled sobs.

"Dad sent me to boarding school so he can keep working," said Oliver.

"What about your mum?" asked Lewis.

"She died."

Lewis didn't know what to say.

Oliver looked glum. "When I first met you, I was unpacking and I felt so lonely. I got a shock when you walked in. I could see you were the boy I'd seen on the playing fields. I knew you were one of those sporty people who are always popular. Then, when you didn't seem to care that you lost the ball, it made me really angry that you could be so careless and just get away with it."

"Is that why you lied to me about having to pay for it and getting expelled?"

"I wasn't really lying. Just exaggerating, I suppose. I thought that if you lost something, you should have to pay for it," said Oliver. "That's what my dad says."

"I didn't know how things worked down here – like putting the ball away. We don't do that where I'm from. And how could I be popular when I didn't know anyone? You were the first person I met at school and you were super unfriendly. It made me really unhappy. It's been hard sharing the room this week," said Lewis.

Oliver stared at Lewis as if he really saw him for the first time. "I'm sorry."

For a moment everyone was silent, then Helen said, "I think we could do with a break. Who would like a hot chocolate?"

Chapter 12
SHARING

When Helen left the room, Lewis cautiously looked over at Oliver.

"Do you like Zoomtron?" he asked.

Oliver nodded.

"I've just been playing with Aiden and Matt. It's good, isn't it?" Lewis said.

"We could play it here," said Oliver.

"I don't have a computer," replied Lewis.

Oliver's eyes widened. "I have two. My dad has a computer company. I have a lot of electronic devices. You can borrow one."

"That would be great!" exclaimed Lewis. "Although, I haven't used computers much. I'm just learning how they work."

"Well, I'm still learning about sport," said Oliver. "I've been avoiding it most of my life."

Lewis laughed. "You know I was only trying to help you before at basketball, don't you?"

Oliver nodded. "I just got that stupid idea in my

head about you. I guess I was looking for someone to blame because I felt miserable. I'm sorry I've made things harder for you."

"You can help make things easier by teaching me about computers," laughed Lewis.

"It's a deal," said Oliver.

Just then, Helen returned with the hot chocolate. "You two seem to be getting on a lot better," she said, sitting down again. She gazed around the room and frowned. "You know, there should be two sets of drawers up here. I'll make sure one gets moved in as soon as possible."

Lewis looked at Oliver and grinned. "That would be awesome! Then I'd have somewhere to put all my mess."

The afternoon and evening went by in a blur of conversation and games. Lewis felt the happiest he'd been since he had arrived at Southward School.

He was exhausted when bedtime came. When they turned the lights out, he knew he wasn't going to have any trouble sleeping.

That night, Lewis dreamt that he was sitting around a campfire in the desert near his home. It was a cold evening and the stars were bright in the sky.

The light of the fire flickered over the faces of his family. He looked around and he could see them all. Oliver was there, too, a part of the group, laughing at a joke Pop had told him.

Tilly, who was sitting next to Lewis, turned to him. She took his hand, and recited an old Aboriginal saying,

"We are all visitors to this time, this place. We are just passing through. Our purpose here is to observe, to learn, to grow, to love … and then we return home."

Lewis woke the next morning feeling good. He knew he was going to get a lot out of being at his new school. He'd experienced so much in just one week. He wondered what the next six years would bring.